PLEASE WASH
YOUR HANDS
BEFORE YOU READ ME
AND KEEP ME CLEAN

BIG BAD GOAT

by Anne Rockwell

A Smart Cat Book

E. P. Dutton   New York

Library of Congress Cataloging in Publication Data

Rockwell, Anne F.   Big Bad Goat.
(A Smart Cat book)

Summary: When Big Strong Dog, Big Strong Sheep, and Big
Strong Horse fail to help Tommy, Little Bee succeeds in
getting Big Bad Goat out of Tommy's yard.
[1. Domestic animals—Fiction.   2. Bees—Fiction]
I. Title. II. Series.
PZ7.R5943Bh [E]   81-12638
ISBN 0-525-45100-5   AACR2

Published in the United States by E. P. Dutton, Inc.,
2 Park Avenue, New York, N.Y. 10016

Published simultaneously in Canada by Clarke,
Irwin & Company Limited, Toronto and Vancouver

Editor: Ann Durell   Designer: Janice Ferro

Printed in the U.S.A.   First Edition
10 9 8 7 6 5 4 3 2 1

Big Bad Goat

got in Tommy's yard.

"Chomp, chomp, chomp!"

It began to eat

the flowers in Tommy's yard.

"Shoo, Big Bad Goat!

Get out!" said Tommy.

But Big Bad Goat

would not go.

7

Tommy saw Big Strong Dog.

"Come with me," said Tommy.

"Shoo Big Bad Goat

out of my yard."

8

But Big Strong Dog

would not come.

It was too scared

of Big Bad Goat.

9

Tommy saw Big Strong Sheep.

"Come with me," said Tommy.

"Shoo Big Bad Goat

out of my yard."

10

But Big Strong Sheep

would not come.

It was too scared

of Big Bad Goat.

Tommy saw Big Strong Horse.

"Come with me," said Tommy.

"Shoo Big Bad Goat

out of my yard."

12

But Big Strong Horse

would not come.

It was too scared

of Big Bad Goat.

13

There was no one

to help Tommy.

14

"Buzz, buzz, buzz,"
said Little Bee.
It smelled honey from
the flowers in Tommy's yard.

16

Little Bee flew around Tommy.

"Buzz, buzz, buzz,"

it said.

17

"Shoo, Little Bee,"
said Tommy.

18

And Little Bee did.

It flew to Big Bad Goat.

20

"Chomp, chomp, chomp!"
went Big Bad Goat
and ate a flower.

21

Little Bee wanted the honey

in that flower.

"Buzz, buzz, buzz!"

it said.

Little Bee stung

Big Bad Goat.

22

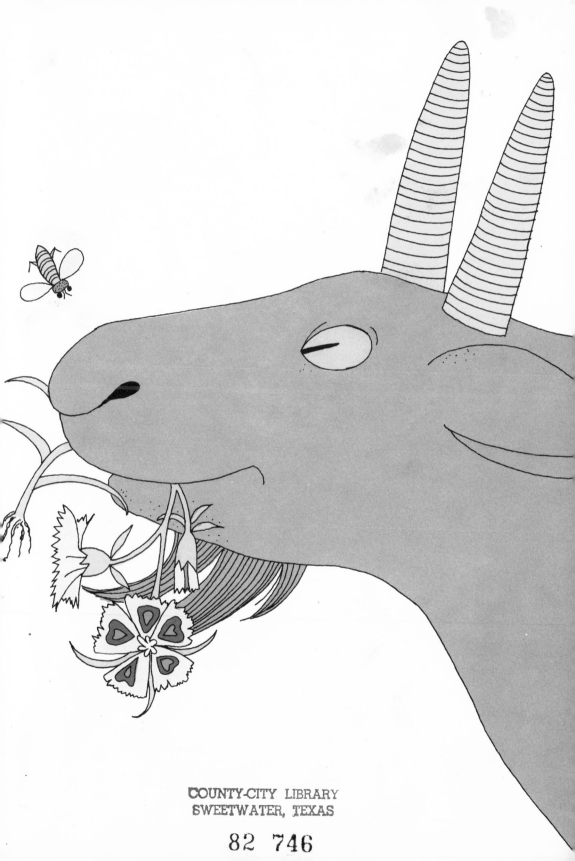

Big Bad Goat got mad.

Big Bad Goat got scared.

24

Big Bad Goat ran away

from Tommy's yard.

26

Little Bee got honey

from all the flowers

in Tommy's yard.

"You are a big help,

Little Bee,"

said Tommy.

"Buzz, buzz, buzz,"

said Little Bee.

And it flew away.